LAYLA
and the BOTS

CUPCAKE FIX

written by
Vicky Fang

BRANCHES
SCHOLASTIC INC.

For "the cousins," my favorite crew to bake with. – VF
To my Studiomates for all your help and support!– CN

Text copyright © 2021 by Vicky Fang
Illustrations copyright © 2021 by Christine Nishiyama

Library of Congress Cataloging-in-Publication Data

Names: Fang, Vicky, author. | Nishiyama, Christine (Illustrator), illustrator.
Title: Cupcake fix / by Vicky Fang ; illustrated by Christine Nishiyama.
Description: First edition. | New York : Branches/Scholastic Inc., 2021. |
Series: Layla and the Bots ; 3 | Audience: Ages 5–7. | Audience: Grades K–1. |
Summary: Blossom Valley is opening a brand-new community center, and Layla and her bots are playing at the opening, but the mayor is worried because not many people have signed up to come to the party; so Layla and her bots decide to build a cupcake machine to attract a crowd—but they are uncertain how to manage the variety of decorations proposed. Includes a DIY activity that readers can try at home.

Identifiers: LCCN 2020006309 (print) |
ISBN 9781338582970 (paperback) | ISBN 9781338582987 (library binding) |
Subjects: LCSH: Robots—Juvenile fiction. | Cupcakes—Juvenile fiction. |
Parties—Juvenile fiction. | CYAC: Robots—Fiction. |
Machinery—Fiction. | Parties—Fiction. | Cupcakes—Fiction.
Classification: LCC PZ7.1.F3543 Ch 2021 (print) | DDC [E]—dc23
LC record available at https://lccn.loc.gov/2020006309

10 9 8 7 6 5 4 3 2 1   21 22 23 24 25

Printed in China   62
First edition, June 2021

Illustrated by Christine Nishiyama
Edited by Rachel Matson
Book design by Maria Mercado

TABLE OF CONTENTS

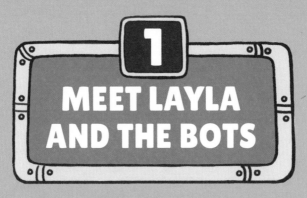

1
MEET LAYLA AND THE BOTS

This is Layla. She is an inventor. And a rock star.

These are the Bots.

BOP

BOOP

BEEP

They are part of Layla's crew.

Beep knows things.

BEEP.
A small motor can make the ball spin.

Boop builds things.

Motor attached.

Bop codes things.

On [POSE] →
DiscoSparkle!

Super shiny!

Layla and the Bots play music in their town of Blossom Valley.

This week, they are playing at the opening of the new community center! This is why they can't stop thinking about group activities . . .

Like picnics,

Yum!

volleyball,

Spike!

and board games.

BEEP. The longest chess game lasted over twenty hours—and nobody won!

5

Whenever Layla and the Bots get together, awesome things happen.

2

OFF-CENTER

On Tuesday morning, Layla and the Bots unpack their gear at the new community center. The big opening is in four days!

This place is great!

BEEP. Now Blossom Valley will have a space for chess tournaments.

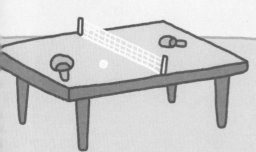

And Ping-Pong playoffs.

And big parties!

Layla sees Mayor Diaz talking to Pam, the community center director. Mayor Diaz looks worried.

Only twelve people are on the guest list for Saturday's opening? I was really hoping for a bigger turnout.

I don't think many people know about the center yet.

BEEP. Sounds like you need to get people excited for Saturday's party.

Yes, but I've tried everything I can think of. I even announced it on TV!

This center has everything the town has been asking for. But if people don't come, we won't be able to keep it open.

Layla pipes up.

We can find a way to get more people to the opening! Right, Bots?

Righto!

Mayor Diaz laughs.

Well, I can't think of a better crew to make this event a hit!

Layla smiles a huge smile.

But what will bring people out to the community center?

3
TASTE TEST

Layla and the Bots sit in the town square to brainstorm.

We need something exciting to bring people out to the event! Any ideas?

BEEP. Food is a good way to bring people together.

Eating, yay!

That's a great idea! But what kind of food would attract a big crowd?

Tacos?

Ice cream.

Brussels sprouts!

Layla and the Bots put together a survey.

The Blossom Valley
Community Center
Opens on Saturday!

What food would you
want to eat there?

☐ tacos   ☐ ice cream
☐ brussels   ☐ other
   sprouts
_____
(Write your suggestion here.)

They hand out the surveys all over town.

At the end of the day, Layla and the Bots have thirty-six completed surveys. They add up the votes.

Tacos got five votes.

Ice cream got ten votes.

Brussels sprouts got— Wanh! One vote?!

And twenty people wrote in "cupcakes"!

Layla makes a graph of the votes.

Blossom Valley's
Favorite Foods
SURVEY RESULTS

NUMBER OF VOTES

20
15
10
5
0

TACOS   ICE CREAM   BRUSSELS SPROUTS   CUPCAKES

Well, Bots, we have our answer! Ready to build a cupcake machine tomorrow?

Whoop—yes!

Inside, Layla's tummy is shaking like strawberry jelly. She knows they can build things . . . but can they BAKE?

4
BAKE-OFF

On Wednesday morning, Layla and the Bots meet in their workshop.

Okay, let's build!

Beep prepares the plans.

Boop gathers the parts.

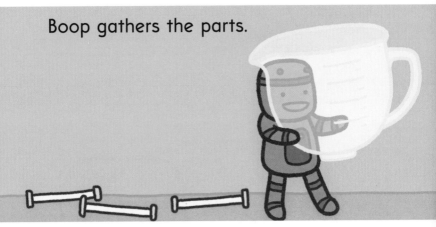

Bop eats jelly beans while his computers boot up.

The machine will have three stations.
First, they build the batter-mixing station.
Beep looks up the ingredients for cupcakes.

Boop builds the mixer.

Bop codes the machine to mix and pour at the right times.

```
mix("30 seconds");
when complete:
pour();
```

Excellent!

Next, they build the baking station.
Beep finds the perfect temperature.

Boop builds the auto-loading oven.
It will put the cupcakes in and take
them out.

Bop codes it to bake for the right amount of time.

on (bake)
{setTimer}
("15 mins")}

Smells delicious!

350°

Finally, they build the frosting station.
Beep measures out the frosting.

Boop builds a twist-and-squeeze
frosting nozzle.

Bop codes the nozzle to frost each cupcake.

The first set of cupcakes comes through the machine. But the cupcakes don't look quite right.

They look a little . . .

Plain?

Bo-ring!

Yes, that.

We need help.

We need pizzazz!

BEEP. We need to learn more about decorating cupcakes.

Layla's eyes sparkle.

5

SWEET DREAMS

The next morning, Layla and the Bots rush to the bakery. Chef Jeff is in the kitchen. He is decorating all sorts of cakes, cookies—and cupcakes!

Chef Jeff! We need your help!

Hi, Layla and the Bots!

Can you show us how to make beautiful cupcakes, like yours?

Chef Jeff smiles. He brings them over to his decorating station.

I always add a special decoration. Like a shiny cherry!

BEEP. That looks yummy.

37

Layla and the Bots leave the bakery with lots of ideas.

SWEET TOOTH BAKERY

So what kind of decoration should we add to our community center cupcakes?

BEEP. Everybody loves a cherry.

Flowers are prettier.

Sprin-kles! Sprin-kles!

Layla wrinkles her brow. Now they have too many ideas. Which one should they pick?

6

MIX IT UP

On the way back to the workshop, Layla and the Bots run into Mayor Diaz and Pam. They are posting flyers for the big opening.

Hi, Layla and the Bots!

The town is buzzing about the cupcake machine you're building! We're up to two hundred guests.

Ooh, big party!

Layla smiles nervously.

It's coming along great! But . . .

But what? Is there a problem?

No! Well, sort of.

Layla explains the three cupcake decoration options.

Layla frowns.

Mayor Diaz and Pam hurry off.

I'm sure you'll figure it out, Layla. See you Saturday!

Layla and the Bots look at one another.

Let people pick?

That means we need three different decorating stations.

And we need to give people a way to pick which one they want!

Layla nods as she draws in her sketchbook.

What about this?

45

CUPCAKE MACHINE

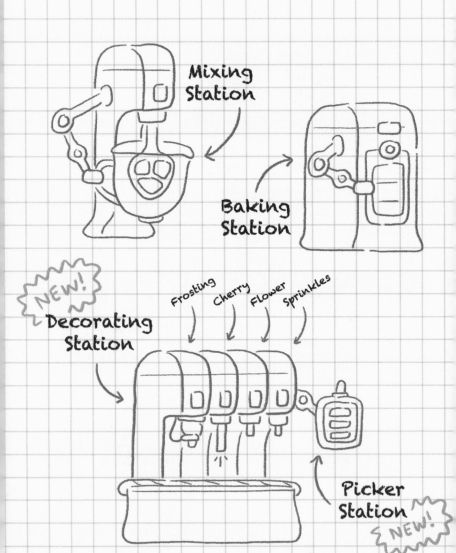

Mixing Station

Baking Station

NEW!

Decorating Station

Frosting Cherry Flower Sprinkles

Picker Station

NEW!

To make a cupcake, first pick your decoration from the screen.

Then the code tells the machine how to decorate the cupcake!

 if (cherry) -->
frost + addCherry!

 if (flower) -->
frost + addFlower!

 if (sprinkles) -->
frost + addSprinkles!

This way, everyone gets to choose their own decoration!

7
RECIPE FOR DISASTER

Layla and the Bots build in their workshop all day on Friday. By the end of the day, they have added three new stations to their machine.

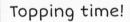

Topping time!

The Cherry Topper places a shiny
cherry on top.

The Petal Pusher squeezes out perfect
sugar flowers.

And the Sprinkle Sprinkler showers rainbow sprinkles.

Finally, Bop adds the code so people can pick the design they want.

Let's test it out!

if (cherry)-->
frost + add cherry!

if (flower)-->
frost + add Flower!

if (sprinkles)-->
frost + add Sprinkles!

Bop presses the sprinkles button. Then the Sprinkle Sprinkler adds the decoration.

Layla and the Bots high five.

Yum!

On Saturday morning, they bring their machine to the community center. Mayor Diaz and Pam are thrilled to see it.

Make your own cupcakes! I love it!

Mayor Diaz steps up to the machine.
She tells the machine to make a cupcake
with a cherry, a flower, <u>and</u> sprinkles.

The machine gurgles and shudders. Then it groans and blasts a frosting explosion!

8
A STICKY SITUATION

The community center is covered in sticky, messy frosting. Layla's eyes fill with tears.

57

It's okay, Layla. You tried your best.

But now we have more than two hundred people coming here in just a few hours. They're looking for cupcakes, and we don't have <u>any</u> to give them!

Layla knows Mayor Diaz is right. Without the cupcake machine, today's opening will be ruined!

They all work together to clean up the mess. But Layla can't stop thinking about what went wrong with the machine! She and the Bots have to find a way to fix it.

I don't understand! The machine worked every time we tested it in the workshop.

Build-Your-Own Cupcake Machine

350°

BEEP. It made cherry cupcakes!

And flower cupcakes!

It made sprinkle cupcakes!

Mayor Diaz asked for <u>all</u> <u>three</u> toppings and then . . .

KA-pow.

61

Wait, that's it! Our machine's code was only set up to handle <u>one</u> decoration per cupcake. There's a bug in our code!

A bug?

BEEP. A mistake. An error. Something wrong.

Layla and Bop work together until they've fixed the code. But will the machine work this time?

9

SWEET SUCCESS

It's time for the big event! The community center is full of people. Layla beams as she looks around at everyone eating cupcakes and playing games.

Welcome to Blossom Valley's brand-new community center! Please enjoy this fantastic cupcake machine—thanks to Layla and the Bots!

We never tested the machine with all three options turned on. When you asked for all the toppings, the machine tried to add triple the frosting! That caused the explosion. So we fixed the code so the machine frosts the cupcakes only one time, no matter how many toppings someone picks.

Mayor Diaz gives Layla a high five.

I think the cupcake machine should be a permanent part of the community center!

That's a great idea! People will be sure to come back for cupcakes.

We could add more flavors!

More toppings!

Yay!

Layla laughs.

Okay, okay! But first, we have a show to perform.

Layla and the Bots jump on stage.
It was their sweetest show ever.

DESIGN AND BUILD YOUR OWN

YOU'LL NEED THE FOLLOWING ITEMS:

- 1 large piece of cardboard
- 4 metal brads (or paper clips)
- 1 piece of cardstock
  (or 2 index cards)
- Scissors
- 1 rubber band
- Small, light household objects, such as marbles and paper clips, ideally different sizes/shapes

STEP 1. BUILD THE ARM

- Cut the cardboard to make four strips about 8 inches long and 1 inch wide. Use scissors (and the help of a grown-up) to poke a hole at the top and the middle of each strip.

- Arrange your strips to form an "xx" pattern, with the punched holes overlapping. Push the brads through all four holes to connect your strips. (If you're using paper clips, unbend half of each paper clip to push it through each hole, then bend it back to hold it in place.)

STEP 2. BUILD THE GRABBER

- Cut a piece of cardstock into a long rectangle about 5 inches long and 2 inches wide. Roll the cardstock to form a cone.

- Tape the overlapping edge to hold the cone together. Cut off the corners sticking out.

GRABBER ARM!

- Repeat so you have 2 cones. These are now your grabber scoops.

- Position the scoops on the ends of the arm as shown below. Point the openings toward each other so they fit together. Tape the scoops to the arm.

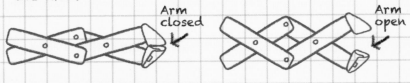

Arm closed

Arm open

STEP 3. TEST AND FIX

- Test out your machine! Can you pick up each of your small, light household objects?

- Try making your grabber scoops different sizes and shapes. Does this improve your design?

STEP 4. ROCK OUT!

- Give your machine a cool name, and draw a picture of your design.

- Decorate your machine.

- Time yourself: How many objects can you place in a bowl in one minute?

HOW MUCH DO YOU KNOW ABOUT CUPCAKE FIX?

Mayor Diaz is worried that people will not come to the party for the community center. How do Layla and the Bots help bring a crowd?

A <u>simile</u> is when you use the words "like" or "as" to compare two unlike things. Can you find the simile on page 23? Write your own simile that describes how Layla's stomach feels.

Why do Layla and the Bots visit Chef Jeff? What ideas come out of this visit?

Reread page 62. What does the phrase "a bug in the code" mean? What is the "bug" in Bop's code?

Layla and the Bots make a survey. Create your own survey to find out your family's or friends' favorite foods! Draw and label a graph of the results. (Hint: Look at the graph on page 21 for ideas.)

ABOUT THE CREATORS

VICKY FANG is a product designer who invents things like buildings that play music and alarm clocks that talk to you. She's never made a cupcake machine . . . but she has made lots of cupcakes! Vicky lives in California with her husband and kids. LAYLA AND THE BOTS is her first children's book series.

CHRISTINE NISHIYAMA is an artist who draws all sorts of stuff in her sketchbook. She's passionate about helping others discover their own way of drawing. Christine lives in North Carolina with her husband, dog, and lil' baby, Butterbean. Christine is also the author and illustrator of the picture book WE ARE FUNGI.

READ MORE

and the

BOOKS!